Materials

These two pages show the variety of art materials that are used in the papercraft projects in this book.

Paper ideas

Below are some of the different papers that are used for the projects. Beneath the heading on most of the pages you'll find a suggestion for the kind of paper to use for that project.

Using a craft knife

Some of the projects suggest using a craft knife to cut out shapes. When you use one, always put a pile of old magazines or one or two pieces of thick cardboard under the paper you are cutting.

Be very careful when you use a craft knife. Keep your fingers away from the blade.

This pink paper has been textured with paint (see pages 6-9).

Patterned wrapping paper

Pages ripped from old magazines

Tissue paper

Corrugated cardboard from an old box. Rip off the top layer of paper to reveal the bumpy surface.

Corrugated cardboard from an art shop

Paper with a raised texture

Art paper is thick and is usually sold in individual sheets.

Scraps of shiny paper from packaging or wrapping paper

Threads

Sequins

Bits and pieces

Some of the projects use bits and pieces that you may have lying around your home. You'll find ideas in this book for printing with erasers and creating collages with found objects.

Threads and sequins are used on pages 32-33, 64-65 and 66-67.

Eraser

Found objects such as washers, press studs and paper fasteners.

Ribbons

Pastels and crayons

There are several projects that use pastels and wax crayons. You can usually buy them in sets.

Wax crayons

Chalk pastels

Paints, inks and pens

A variety of different paints are used in the projects. The step-by-step instructions tell you what type to use.

Acrylic paints can be used straight from their tube or container.

Several projects use a dip pen. If you don't have one, use a fountain pen.

Felt-tip pens

Creating textured paper

Several of the projects in this book, including the paper weaving on pages 28-29 and the 3-D bugs on pages 60-61, use pieces of paper which have been textured by using different paint techniques.

Experiment with the examples on the following four pages to create your own papers.

Wax resist

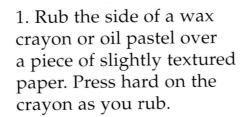

1. Rub the side of a wax crayon or oil pastel over a piece of slightly textured paper. Press hard on the crayon as you rub.

2. Mix some water with paint and brush it over the paper. The wax will resist the paint, leaving the texture of the paper.

Brushmarks

1. Dip a thick household paintbrush in yellow paint, then brush it in stripes across a piece of white paper.

2. Mix some red with the yellow to make orange. Brush it lightly across the yellow paint so that you leave brushmarks.

3. While the paint is still wet, brush red paint on top of the yellow and orange paint, leaving marks as before.

These papers have been textured using the techniques shown above.

Swirly circles

1. Dip a dry, broad paintbrush into thick acrylic paint so that the paint just covers the tips of the bristles.

2. Brush the paint around and around on a piece of paper, pressing hard. You should get lots of individual brushmarks.

3. Dip the tips of the bristles into the paint again and brush another circle beside the first one. Do this again and again.

Sponge marks

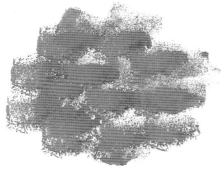

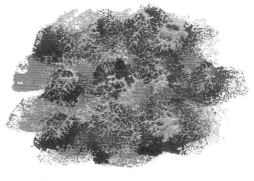

1. Dip a piece of sponge into some paint, then dab it onto a piece of paper. Dip it into the paint each time you dab it on.

2. Then, dab a darker shade of paint over the top of it, leaving some of the original paint showing through.

3. You can even sponge a third shade on top, or dab on some gold or silver acrylic paint, if you have some.

The paper below has been textured by sponging blue paint onto white paper.

More texturing ideas

These pages give you some more examples of how you can create textured papers to use in your projects.

This paper was created by dropping blobs of ink onto wet paper.

This rubbing was done with yellow wax crayon on the large holes of a cheese grater. The rubbing was then painted with ink.

This rubbing was done on the small holes on a cheese grater.

For this effect, sprinkle salt onto wet watery paint. Let it dry, then rub off all the salt.

Paint a piece of plastic foodwrap with paint. Lay a piece of paper on top. Rub lightly over the paper, then lift it off.

This background was also done with paint on plastic foodwrap (see below left).

These pieces were painted with a household paintbrush. Paint on one shade of paint, then brush another shade on top when dry.

This paper was painted with watery paints. It was then spattered with clean water while the paint was wet. Pages 30-31 show you how to spatter.

Rub the side of a wax crayon over a piece of paper then paint it all over.

7

Textured paper picture

BLACK PAPER AND SMALL PIECES OF WHITE PAPER

The steps on this page show you different ways of making textured paper and patterns with paint, pastels and collage. You don't need to follow the ideas exactly, just experiment with the different techniques. You could then cut your samples into squares and then glue them together to make a picture.

1. Follow the steps on page 7 to paint a swirly circle with light blue or ultramarine paint.
Use a thick paintbrush.

2. Paint another piece of paper with blue paint. When it's dry, cut it into strips and glue them onto a piece of white paper.

3. Use a chalk pastel or oil pastel to scribble thick lines across a piece of paper. Do it quickly and don't try to be too neat.

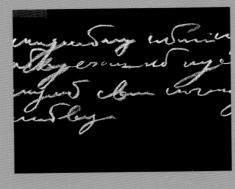

4. Use a white chalk pastel to write long lines of flowing, joined-up writing across a piece of black paper.

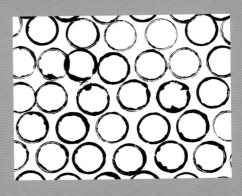

5. Spread black paint on an old saucer, then dip a bottle top into it. Use the bottle top to print several rows of circles.

6. Paint two blue lines across some paper. Glue on two strips which have been painted with black paint. Add a pink square.

7. Use paint to fill in blocks of blue on a piece of paper. Use a chalk pastel to draw a white line across the middle.

8. Cut the pieces of textured paper into rough squares. Arrange them on a large piece of black paper, then glue them on.

1. Rip some strips of blue tissue paper. Glue them across a piece of paper, making them overlap.

2. Cut some thin strips of green tissue paper for the stems and glue them at the bottom of the paper.

3. Cut out some red petals. Glue four petals around the top of some of the stems.

4. Cut out some orange petals. Glue them around other stems, overlapping some of the red petals.

5. Use a thin felt-tip pen to draw a line around each petal. It doesn't need to be too accurate.

6. Draw a small circle in the middle of each flower, then add two or three lines to each petal.

These flowers also have outlines drawn along their stems.

Textured houses

THIN WHITE CARDBOARD

1. Cut a zigzag at one end of a strip of cardboard. Then, paint a rectangle of acrylic paint on another piece of cardboard.

2. Drag the zigzag end of the cardboard across the paint again and again to make textured lines. Leave the paint to dry.

3. Cut several small triangles into the end of another cardboard strip. Drag it across another rectangle of paint.

4. For a very fine texture, drag the end of an old toothbrush across a rectangle of paint, again and again.

5. Do some more textured patches of paint by experimenting with different shapes cut into strips of cardboard.

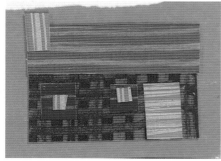

6. Cut rectangles from the textures for the buildings, windows, doors and roofs. Glue them on another piece of cardboard.

Knot the threads tightly around a cord to stop them from moving around.

Folded stars

THICK PAPER

1. Cut several strips from thick paper. Make them the same width. Paint all of the strips the same shade.

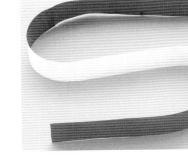

2. Glue the strips of paper together to make one really long strip which is at least three times the width of this single page.

3. Start by folding one end of the strip over, like this. Crease the fold well. The fold will form one edge of the star.

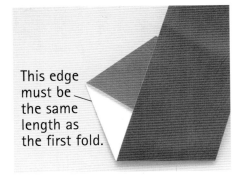

This edge must be the same length as the first fold.

4. Now, fold the long end of the strip upwards, so that the left-hand edge is <u>exactly</u> the same length as the first folded edge.

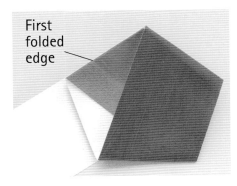

First folded edge

5. Then, fold the paper behind, making sure that it runs along the first folded edge. All the edges should be the same length.

6. Continue folding the long strip around the five-sided shape, making sure that all the edges and folds match neatly.

If you're making lots of stars decorate them in different ways, like the ones shown here.

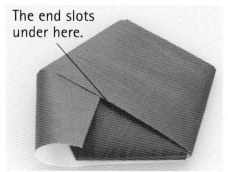

The end slots under here.

Don't be afraid to press the edges quite hard.

Be careful as you push the needle through.

7. When you reach the end of the long strip, push the loose end under the strip as far as it will go and crease its fold.

8. Press in each side of the shape firmly to make a rough star shape. Then, pinch each point in turn to make them neat.

9. Decorate the star with paint or glitter glue. Then, push a needle and thread through one point and tie the ends to make a loop.

17

Cardboard collage

CARDBOARD AND TEXTURED PAPERS (SEE PAGES 6-9)

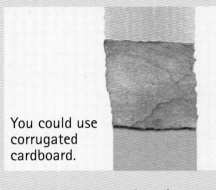

You could use corrugated cardboard.

1. Rip a rectangle of cardboard and one from paper, painted blue. Cut a rectangle from cardboard, then glue them together.

2. Rip triangular shapes from textured paper. Then, glue them on the top piece of cardboard, making a zigzag shape.

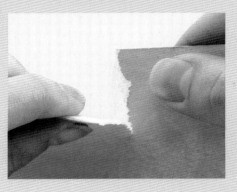

3. Rip another rectangle of painted paper. Hold it in one hand and tear it up towards you. This gives a pale, ripped edge.

The ripped blue paper is under here.

4. Glue on the painted rectangle, then glue pale tissue paper on top so that the ripped edges show. Add a blue dot.

5. Rip two spirals in a piece of silver paper. Then, use scissors to cut beside the ripped edges to make thin spiral strips.

6. Glue the silver spirals onto the painted paper. Then, rip a rectangle from red paper and glue it beside them.

18

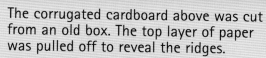

This collage was made using corrugated cardboard and a variety of textured paper.

The corrugated cardboard above was cut from an old box. The top layer of paper was pulled off to reveal the ridges.

This black paper was from photocopied paper.

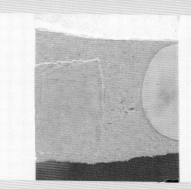

7. Glue a black rectangle across the bottom of the cardboard and glue a strip of paper, ripped from a magazine, on top.

8. Rip a blue rectangle and an orange circle from textured paper. Glue them on, wrapping any spare paper around to the back.

9. Rip a thin strip of black paper. Glue it on so that it overlaps the red stripe, the blue rectangle and the tissue paper above.

Paper mosaic tins

WHITE PAPER, LONG ENOUGH TO WRAP AROUND A TIN

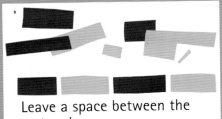

Leave a space between the rectangles.

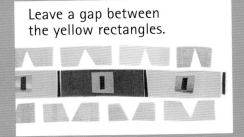

Leave a gap between the yellow rectangles.

1. Cut a rectangle of white paper the same height as a tin. Cut pieces of green paper and glue them along the middle of the paper.

2. Glue thin strips of red paper between the rectangles. Glue purple strips onto yellow squares, then glue them on top.

3. Cut rectangles from yellow paper, then cut a 'V' shape in each one. Glue them in a line, either side of the green strip.

All the paper used on these mosaic tins came from magazine pages.

You could use this technique to make a bookmark.

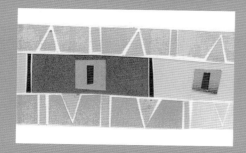 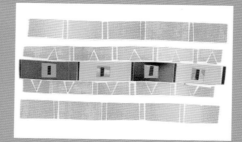 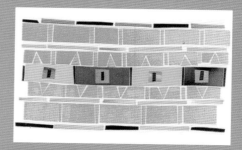

4. Cut triangles and thin strips from another shade of green paper and glue them in the spaces in the yellow rectangles.

5. Add two more lines of yellow rectangles and green strips. This time, leave a slightly wider space between the lines.

6. Glue thin yellow and green strips of paper in the spaces you left. Then, add green and red strips at the top and bottom.

These tins are ideal to use as a container for pens and pencils.

7. Cut a piece of book covering film large enough to cover the mosaic. Peel off the backing paper and smooth it on.

8. Wrap the paper around the tin and trim the ends so that it fits exactly. Tape the ends together to secure them.

Tissue paper pond

TISSUE PAPER

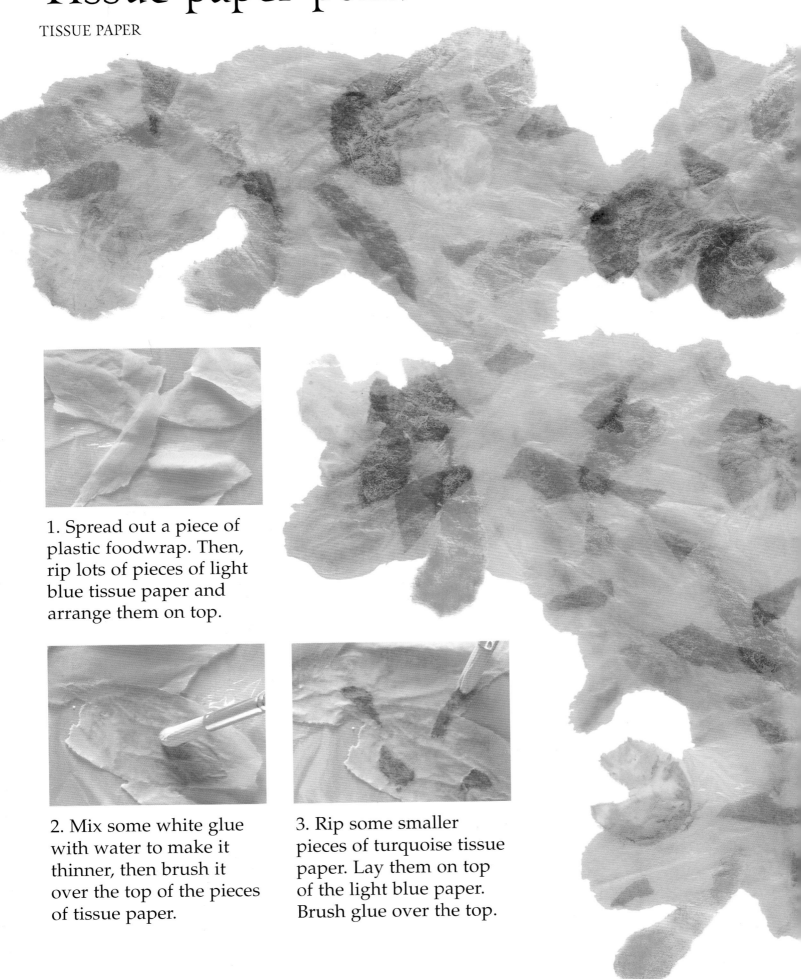

1. Spread out a piece of plastic foodwrap. Then, rip lots of pieces of light blue tissue paper and arrange them on top.

2. Mix some white glue with water to make it thinner, then brush it over the top of the pieces of tissue paper.

3. Rip some smaller pieces of turquoise tissue paper. Lay them on top of the light blue paper. Brush glue over the top.

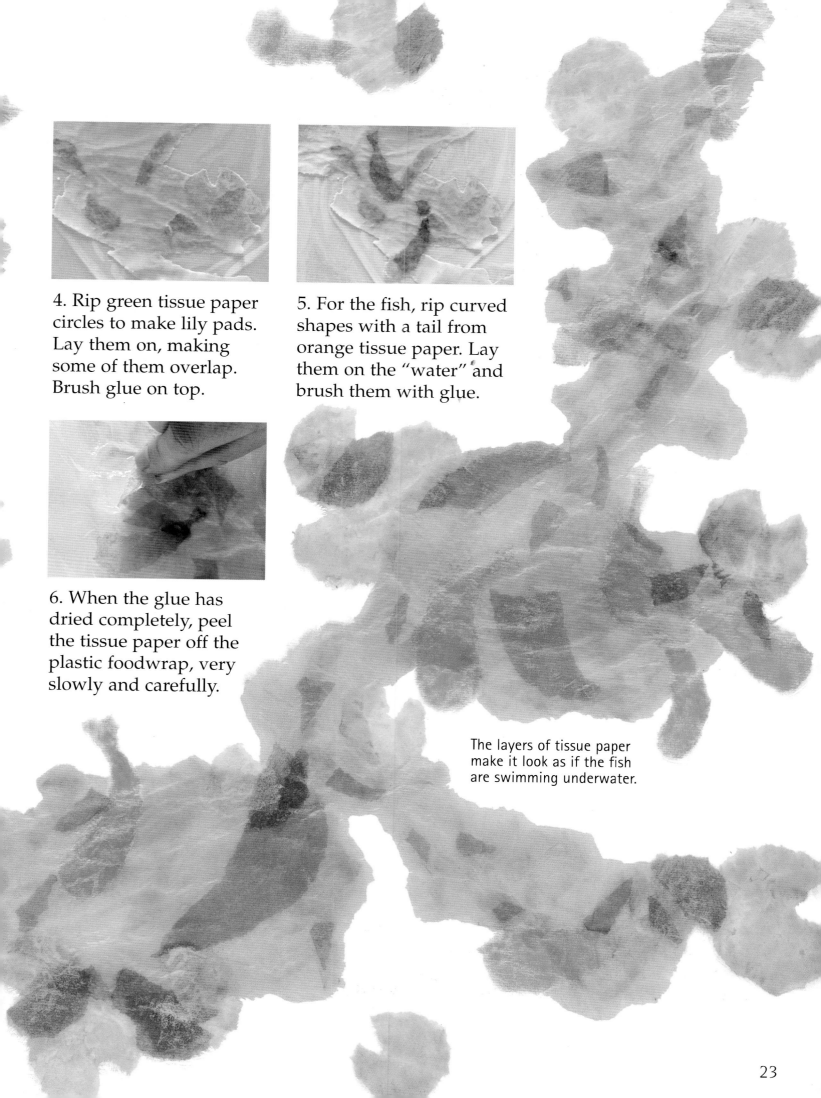

4. Rip green tissue paper circles to make lily pads. Lay them on, making some of them overlap. Brush glue on top.

5. For the fish, rip curved shapes with a tail from orange tissue paper. Lay them on the "water" and brush them with glue.

6. When the glue has dried completely, peel the tissue paper off the plastic foodwrap, very slowly and carefully.

The layers of tissue paper make it look as if the fish are swimming underwater.

Wacky faces

CORRUGATED CARDBOARD AND BRIGHT PAPER

1. Draw a simple outline of a face on a piece of scrap paper. Draw a line down the middle with a shape for a nose, like this.

2. Trace your drawing onto tracing paper. Then, turn the tracing over and scribble over the lines with your pencil.

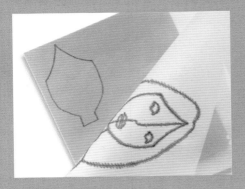

3. Turn the tracing over, then use a ballpoint pen to draw over the outline of the face onto some pale paper. Cut it out.

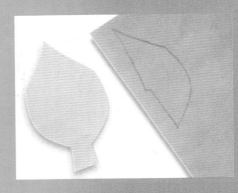

4. Lay the tracing onto some darker paper. Draw over the outline of the right-hand side of the face only and cut it out.

Use a craft knife to cut out the hair.

5. Trace the hair onto thin cardboard and cut it out. Place some corrugated cardboard behind the hole and secure it with tape.

6. Glue the face onto the hair. Then, glue on the right side of the face. Cut out, and glue on, lips and eyes. Draw on eyelashes.

7. Cut out a sweater from another piece of cardboard and glue it on top so that it overlaps the hair and neck.

Male face

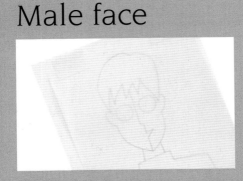

1. Follow steps 1 to 4. Then, trace the whole outline onto cardboard and cut it out. Tape black cardboard behind.

2. Glue the right side onto the face, then use a craft knife to cut the eyes. Glue the face onto the corrugated cardboard.

This girl's
sweater was
cut out of the
background.

This corrugated
cardboard was
bought in an
art shop.

Paper weaving

ANY KIND OF PAPER

Make the slits
a finger-width
apart.

1. Draw a pencil line
across one end of a
rectangle of paper. Cut
lots of slits up to the
line you have drawn.

2. Cut lots of strips of
different shades of paper.
Make them longer than
the width of the rectangle
in step 1.

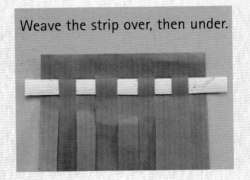

Weave the strip over, then under.

3. Weave one strip of
paper in and out of the
slits in the rectangle.
Then, push it up against
the top of the slits.

4. Weave another strip
below the first one. If the
first strip started 'over'
the cut strip, then the
second starts 'under' it.

5. Continue weaving the
strips until you have
filled the rectangle. Push
each strip against the one
above it, as you go.

6. Turn your weaving over
and use a piece of tape to
secure the strips. Then,
cut off the extra paper
above the pencil line.

These two weavings used a
mixture of wrapping paper and
paper with a raised texture.

The weaving above used plastic from different plastic bags.

Try weaving pieces of ribbon and string between the paper strips.

You could cut a frame from cardboard (see page 54) and tape a paper weaving behind it.

This weaving had wavy slits cut in the rectangle, with straight strips woven through.

For a weaving like the one below, cut different widths of slits in the rectangle.

27

Woven hearts and stars

TEXTURED PAPER (SEE PAGES 6-9)

Don't cut right to the edges of the heart.

1. Cut a large heart from a piece of textured paper or thin cardboard. Then, cut slits down the heart with a craft knife.

2. Cut a strip of textured paper and weave it through the slits. Then, push it up towards the top of the heart.

3. Weave another strip below the first one. Make sure that you weave it over and under in the opposite way to the strip above.

Cut slits down a star. Weave short strips across the top and bottom points.

4. Continue weaving shorter and shorter strips of paper until you have filled the bottom part of the heart.

The orange strips woven through this star were cut in different widths.

5. To fill the top of the heart, cut four short strips of paper. Weave them at a slight angle, like this.

6. When the heart is completely filled, trim the ends off the strips, a little way away from the edges of the heart.

Spattered paper collage

BRIGHT PAPER, SUCH AS ART PAPER

Weight the newspaper with small stones.

1. This can be quite messy so do this outdoors. Put your paper onto some newspapers.

2. Put some ready-mix paint into a container. Add water to make it runny.

3. Dip an old toothbrush into the paint. Then, hold the brush over the paper.

4. Pull a ruler along the brush towards you, so the paint spatters onto the paper.

5. Keep spattering more paint on top until you get the effect you want. Let it dry.

6. Mix another shade of paint and spatter it in the same way on top of the first one.

7. To get big spatters, dip a household paintbrush into runny paint.

8. Flick the brush sharply downwards over the paper. Repeat with more paint.

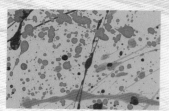   

9. Continue flicking the paint until you have the pattern you want. Leave it to dry.

10. Draw the outline of a frog and leaves on the back of the spattered paper.

11. Draw some plants and a strip for water on the finely spattered paper.

12. Cut out the paper shapes and glue them onto a piece of contrasting paper.

Sparkling squares

TRANSPARENT BOOK COVERING FILM

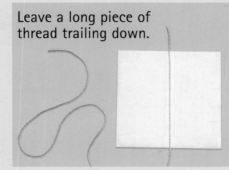

Leave a long piece of thread trailing down.

1. Cut two squares of book covering film, the same size. Peel the backing paper off one of them and lay it sticky-side up.

2. Cut a long piece of bright thread and lay it across the film, like this. It will stick to the sticky surface.

The shapes sparkle as they turn.

3. Rip lots of small pieces of tissue paper. Then, press them onto the film, leaving spaces in between them.

4. Press different shapes of sequins into the gaps between the paper. You could add some pieces of ribbon or thread, too.

Lay the thread on the film at different angles.

5. Peel the backing paper off the other piece of film and press it over the decorated piece. Then, trim the edges.

6. Attach more squares of book film below the first one, leaving some thread showing between the squares.

These squares of film were stitched together.

You could add glitter for some extra sparkle.

33

Fashion cut-outs

ART PAPER AND WRAPPING PAPER

1. Cut out a page from an old magazine with a photograph or drawing of a figure wearing an outfit.

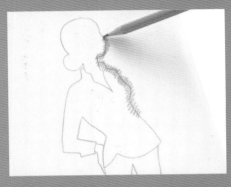

2. Trace a simple outline of the head, body and clothes. Then, turn the tracing over and scribble pencil over the lines.

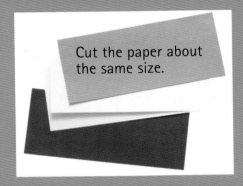

Cut the paper about the same size.

3. Cut two pieces of white paper, one brown piece and one pink. Make them larger than your figure drawing.

Press firmly.

4. Lay the tracing, shaded-side down, onto the brown paper. Draw around the head, feet and hand with a ballpoint pen.

5. Cut them out with a craft knife, keeping all the shapes. Trace the clothes onto the pink paper and cut them out.

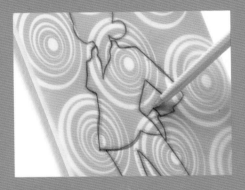

6. Lay your tracing onto a piece of wrapping paper. Draw around the clothes again, then cut them out.

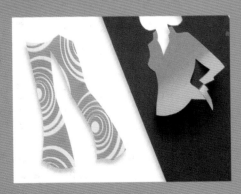

7. Glue the large piece of brown paper onto one of the pieces of white paper. Glue the pink shirt and patterned bottoms on top.

8. Glue the patterned shirt onto the other piece of white paper. Then, glue the large piece of pink paper on top.

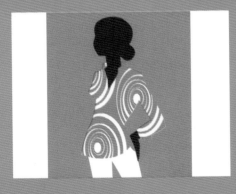

9. Then, glue the brown head, hand and feet onto the figure on the pink paper. (You don't use the pink bottoms at all).

Glue your pictures side by side
on a large piece of paper.

If you can't find
a suitable picture
in a magazine,
trace over one
of these figures.

Folded dyed paper

WHITE OR LIGHT SHADES OF TISSUE PAPER

1. Fold a rectangle of tissue paper about the size of this page in half. Then, fold it in half three more times.

2. Dip a paintbrush in clean water and paint it all over the folded paper. Do this again and again until the paper is damp.

3. Paint a band of blue ink across the middle of the paper. Do this two or three times so that the ink soaks into the paper.

The paper below had blobs of ink painted all over it when it was folded.

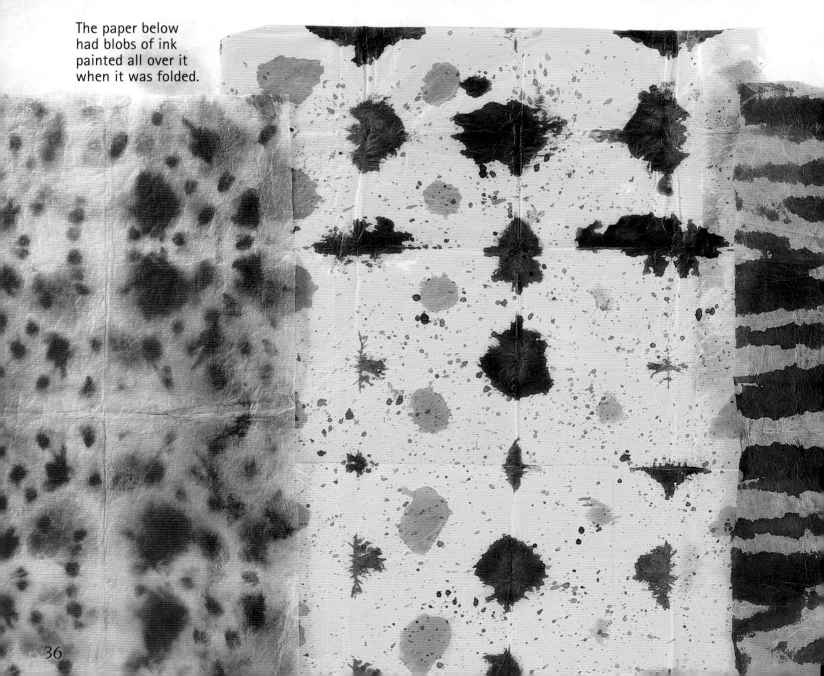

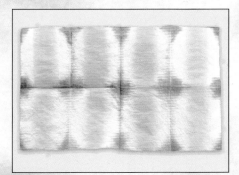

4. Paint each corner of the folded paper with purple ink. Let the ink soak into the paper and mix with the blue ink.

5. Leave the folded paper to dry. When it is completely dry, unfold it very carefully to reveal the dyed pattern.

6. Dip a paintbrush into purple ink. Hold it above the paper and flick the bristles of the brush to splatter the ink all over.

This green paper had lots of stripes painted across it.

Paper shapes

ANY KIND OF PAPER

Spiral

1. Cut a circle from bright paper, then draw a spiral from the edge of the circle to the middle of it.

2. At the middle of the circle, curve the line around a little, then draw another line out to the edge of the circle.

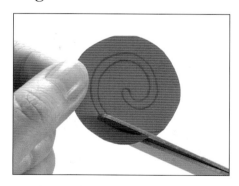

3. Cut along one of the lines of the spiral, turning the paper as you cut. Continue cutting until you reach the edge again.

4. Cut the pointed end off the spiral and trim any wobbly parts from around the edges. Glue it onto another shade of paper.

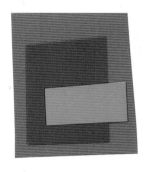

Build up layers of different shapes on top of each other.

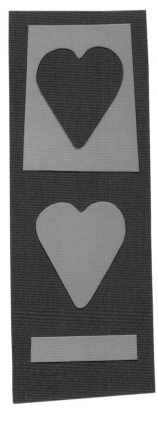

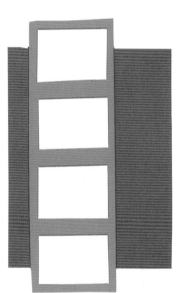

For a sun, cut a circle, then cut small triangles out of its edge. Glue another circle on top.

38

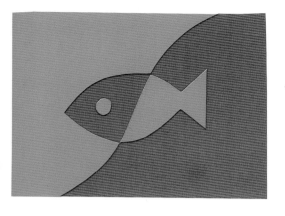

The shapes below could be used on a Valentine's card.

Fish

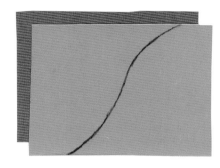

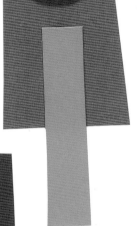

Try combining rounded shapes with squares and rectangles.

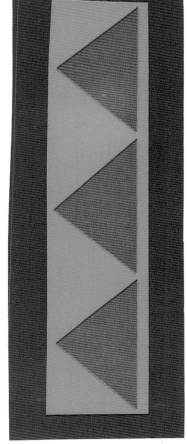

1. Cut two rectangles, the same size, from blue and orange paper. Then, draw a wavy line across the blue one.

2. Draw a simple outline of a fish across the line. Cut along the line, then cut out the front part of the fish, like this.

3. Glue the front part onto the orange rectangle. Then, cut out the back of the blue fish and glue it on. Glue on a blue eye.

Giraffe collage

A LARGE PIECE OF CARDBOARD

Don't glue these areas yet.

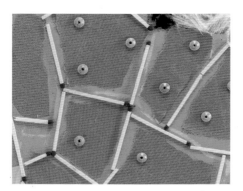

1. Glue a piece of brown wrapping paper onto some cardboard. Then, rip another piece of paper. Glue it across the bottom.

2. Cut out a giraffe's body and legs. Cut a head from corrugated cardboard. Glue the pieces to the background, like this.

3. Rip lots of patches from brown paper and glue them onto the body. Glue matchsticks around them. Add beads or dried beans.

4. Glue fluffy feathers or lots of pieces of wool or yarn down the neck for the mane. Glue long feathers over the top.

5. Wrap black wool or yarn around each hoof and glue on things like matchsticks, feathers and pieces of shiny paper.

6. For the giraffe's antlers, twist the wire off an old peg. Glue a large, dried seed or bean onto the end of each peg.

Make birds to glue around the giraffe by ripping a paper body and wing. Join them with a paper fastener.

7. For eyes, glue together things such as feathers, dried plants and buttons. Stick them on, then stick the rest of the body down.

Don't worry if you don't have exactly the objects shown on this picture - use whatever you can find.

The tail was tucked underneath the body before the body was stuck down.

Mosaic patterns

1. Cut small rectangles of thick white paper. Paint each one with a different shade of blue ink or paint. Leave them to dry.

2. Cut about ten long, thin triangles from one of the painted papers. Glue them in a circle on a piece of white paper.

These were made up from different patterns of triangles, rectangles and semicircles.

3. Cut little triangles from a different piece of painted paper and glue them around the edge of the circle, like this.

4. Cut several small rectangles and glue them around the circle. Space them out evenly between the triangles.

5. Glue a long, thin triangle in between the rectangles. Then, glue two even thinner triangles on either side.

6. Cut small triangles and glue them in a star shape at the end of the thin triangles. Make the points touch the middle triangle.

7. To finish the mosaic pattern, cut long, thin triangles and glue them at the end of each of the small rectangles.

43

Embossed circles

THIN CARDBOARD AND ART PAPER

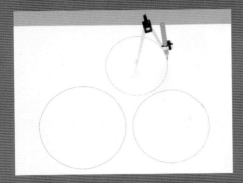

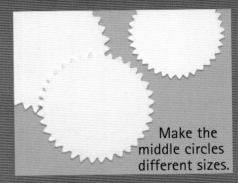

Make the
middle circles
different sizes.

1. Use a pair of compasses
to draw three circles on
a piece of thin cardboard.
Make each one a slightly
different size.

2. Draw a wavy edge
around each circle and a
plain circle in the middle
of each one. Cut around
the wavy lines.

3. In the middle of the
largest circle, draw
curved shapes. Then,
carefully use a craft knife
to cut them out.

4. Use a hole puncher to
punch holes in some
scraps of cardboard. Open
the puncher and glue the
circles around the edge.

5. Cut the middle out
of one of the other circles
and cut a wavy line
around it. Then, cut a
circle out of its middle.

7. Glue another wavy-
edged circle onto the
remaining circle. Cut out
a ring of cardboard and
glue it in the middle.

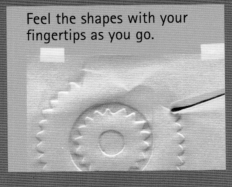

Feel the shapes with your
fingertips as you go.

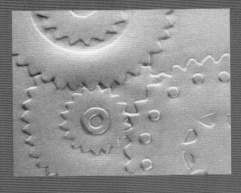

7. Lay all the pieces onto
some paper or cardboard.
Arrange them in an
overlapping pattern, then
glue them on.

8. Tape a piece of art
paper over the circles.
Use the end of a teaspoon
to press and rub around
the cardboard shapes.

9. Continue pressing
around the shapes until
you have revealed all the
shapes. This technique
is called 'embossing'.

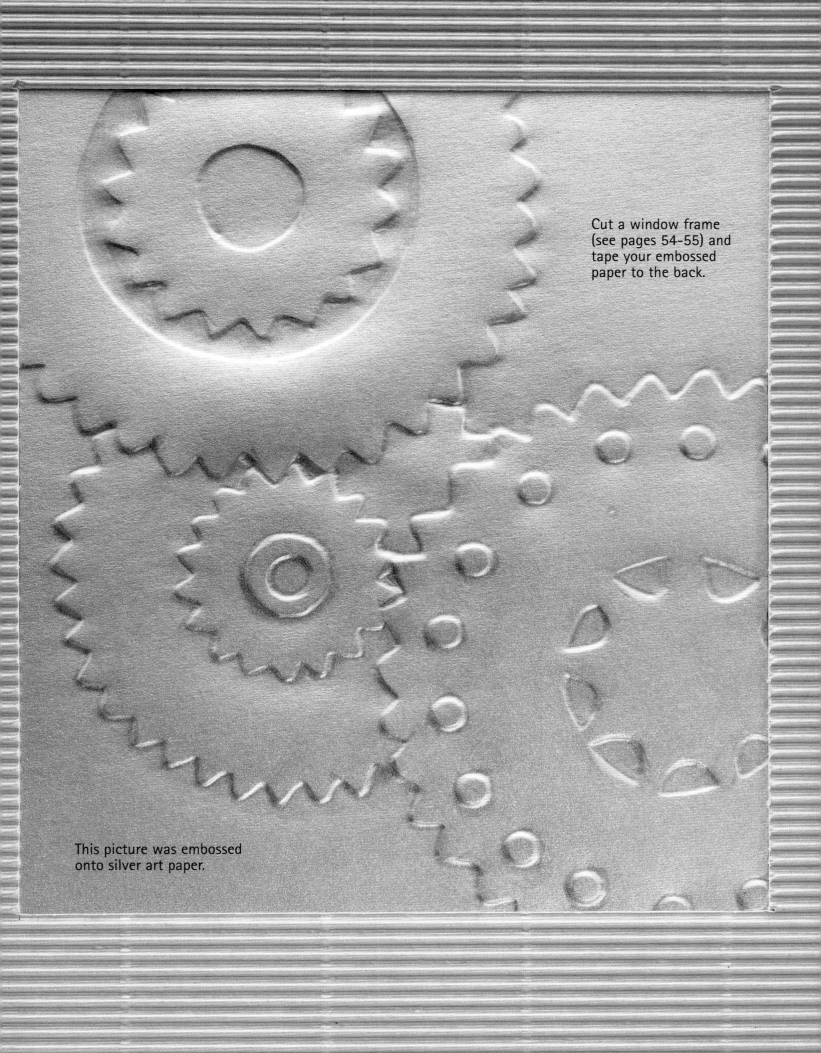

Cut a window frame
(see pages 54–55) and
tape your embossed
paper to the back.

This picture was embossed
onto silver art paper.

Leaf collage
THICK PAPER OR CARDBOARD

1. Use dark paint and a thick paintbrush to paint vertical and horizontal lines on your paper.

2. When the paint has dried, cut a piece of tissue paper to cover the lines, and glue it on.

3. Rip some squares and rectangles from different shades of tissue paper and glue them on.

4. Cut a square of corrugated cardboard. Press it into some paint and print it several times.

5. Either cut out leaves from a picture in a magazine, or cut some leaf shapes from paper.

6. Cut small rectangles from a magazine picture of leaves or grass. Glue them on.

7. Add some horizontal and vertical lines with a felt-tip pen. Then, outline the leaves, loosely.

Geometric prints

ANY PAPER

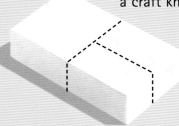

Be very careful when cutting with a craft knife.

1. Use a craft knife to cut a long eraser in half. Then, cut one of the pieces of eraser in half lengthways.

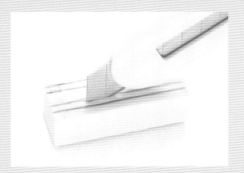

2. Draw sets of parallel lines along the eraser. Then, holding the knife at an angle, make a clean cut along one line.

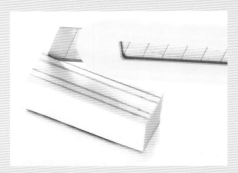

3. Turn the eraser around and cut along the other side of the line to make a groove. Cut the other line in the same way.

4. Cut the corners off the other half of the eraser to make a triangle. Draw four lines on it, then cut along them as before.

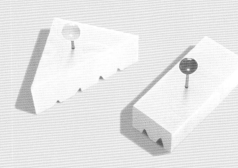

5. Push a map pin or an ordinary pin into the back of both pieces of eraser. This makes them easier to hold when you print.

6. Wet a piece of sponge cloth, then squeeze out as much water as you can. Spread acrylic paint on it with the back of a spoon.

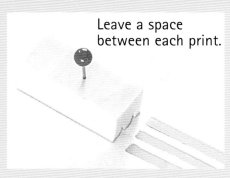

Leave a space between each print.

7. Press the first eraser into the paint, then onto some paper. Press it in the paint again before you do another print.

8. Then, do a triangle print above each set of line prints. Repeat these rows of prints several times on your paper.

9. Cut a small square of eraser and print it between each triangle. Then, cut a line across another square of eraser and print it on top.

These geometric patterns were built up
using erasers cut into different shapes.

Busy street collage

OLD MAGAZINES AND BRIGHT OR TEXTURED PAPER (SEE PAGES 6-9)

1. Cut lots of different textures from magazines. Cut pieces of hair, ears and lips from photos of people, too.

2. Draw a hairstyle on a piece of paper with hair texture and cut it out. Glue it onto a small piece of white paper.

3. Lay tracing paper over the hair and draw a face and neck to fit it. Turn the tracing over and rub pencil over the lines.

To make a street scene, use the ideas shown here to make lots of figures. Glue them onto a background.

Instead of a wall, you could cut out textures of plants and glue them on to make a hedge.

Press firmly.

Add other details, like a teddy bear.

4. Turn the tracing back over. Lay it on top of some paper with a skin tone. Draw over the face again, then cut it out.

5. Glue the face on the hair. Cut out a mouth and ear, then draw eyes and a nose. Cut a dress from textured paper and glue it on.

6. Cut out legs, arms and a pair of shoes and glue them on. Add a sleeve at the top of the arm and a heart-shaped pocket.

Tissue paper fish

TISSUE PAPER

Draw a square around it.

1. Use a thick black felt-tip pen to draw a bold drawing of a fish. Do it on white paper.

2. Trace the main shapes of your fish onto different shades of tissue paper, then cut them out.

Use your picture as a guide.

3. Cut a piece of polythene from a clear plastic bag. Make sure it is bigger than your drawing.

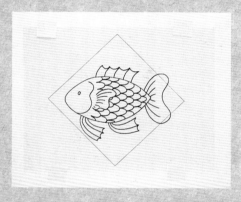

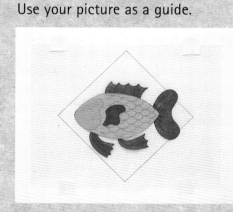

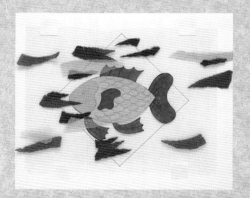

4. Lay the polythene over your drawing. Put pieces of tape along the edges to secure it.

5. Brush the tissue paper shapes with white glue. Press each one in place onto the polythene.

6. Cut or tear strips of tissue paper for the background. Glue them on around the fish.

7. Glue a piece of pale blue tissue paper over the whole picture, then leave it to dry.

8. When the glue is completely dry, carefully peel the tissue paper off the polythene.

9. Place the tissue paper over your drawing. Go over your outlines using black paint.

Your picture will
be stronger if
you cut a frame
and glue it onto
the picture.

These pictures
look especially
good if you
hang them
in a window.

Making frames

On the next four pages you can find out how to make different types of frames for your pictures.

When you make a frame, choose a piece of cardboard which will go well with the picture you are framing. If you decide to decorate your frame, don't make it too elaborate, otherwise your picture will be swamped.

This simple frame was made from strips of corrugated cardboard.

Simple strip frame

1. Cut a piece of cardboard the size you want your frame to be. Glue your picture in the middle of it.

2. Cut two strips of cardboard for the top and bottom of the frame. Make sure they overlap your picture a little.

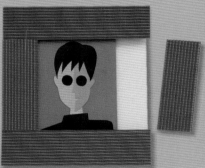

3. For the sides of the frame, cut two pieces of cardboard which fit between the top and bottom strips.

4. Glue on the top strip of cardboard, then the two sides and finally the bottom strip to complete the frame.

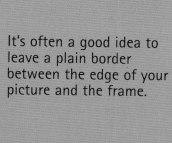

It's often a good idea to leave a plain border between the edge of your picture and the frame.

A square 'window' frame

1. Cut two squares of cardboard the size you want the frame. Then, lay your picture on one of the squares.

2. Use a pencil to draw around your picture. This will give you a guide for the size for the 'window' you'll cut into the frame.

3. Draw another shape about 5mm (¼ in.) inside the pencil lines. Then, place the cardboard on an old magazine.

4. Cut along the inside shape with a craft knife. Cut each line several times rather than trying to cut through first time.

5. Lay the frame over your picture. Turn them over and attach the picture with pieces of tape. Then, erase any pencil lines.

6. Glue the frame onto the spare cardboard square. Put a heavy pile of books on top until the glue has dried.

More frame ideas

These two pages show ideas for decorating the strip frame and window frame shown on the previous two pages.

Glue lots of pieces of ripped tissue paper to make a frame like this orangey-red one.

The picture it is framing had lines painted with acrylic paint. Then, chalk pastel patterns were added when the paint was dry.

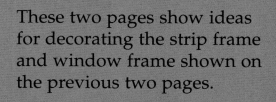

This corrugated cardboard frame was cut from an old box. It was painted with acrylic paint, then rubbed with sandpaper when the paint was dry.

The line around the window was drawn with a gold felt-tip pen.

This picture is a cardboard collage (see pages 18-19).

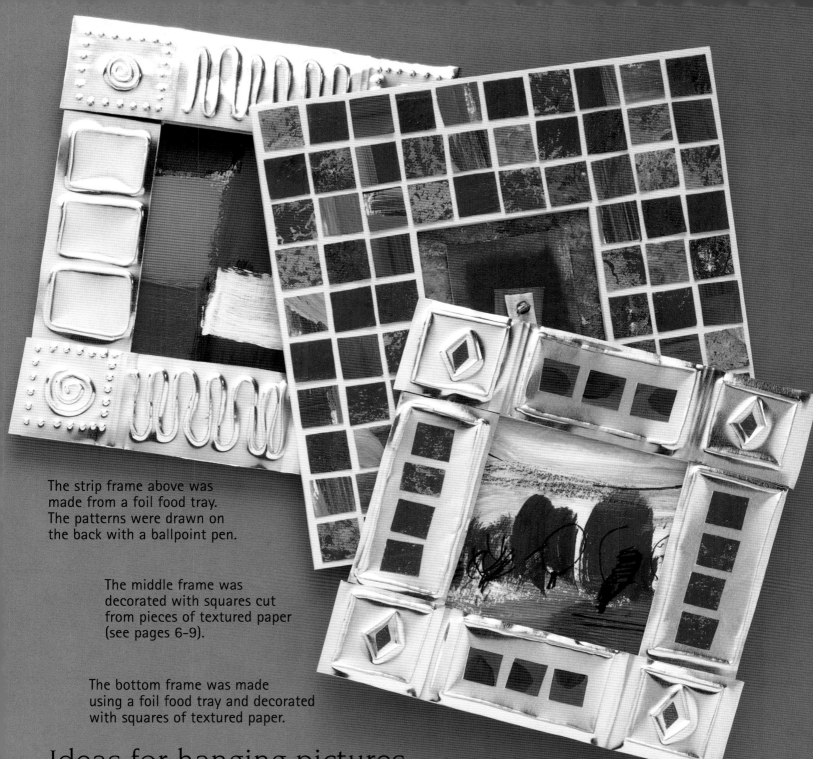

The strip frame above was made from a foil food tray. The patterns were drawn on the back with a ballpoint pen.

The middle frame was decorated with squares cut from pieces of textured paper (see pages 6–9).

The bottom frame was made using a foil food tray and decorated with squares of textured paper.

Ideas for hanging pictures

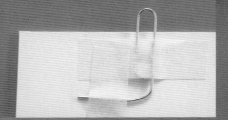

Bend this side upwards.

For a loop hanger, cut a piece of thin string and use a piece of strong tape to attach it to the back of your frame.

For a metal hanger, unbend the end of a paperclip. Use several pieces of strong tape to attach it to the frame.

To make a stand, cut a triangle from cardboard and fold it in half. Cut the bottom edges at an angle, then glue on one half.

Simple figures

THICK BRIGHT PAPER OR CARDBOARD

1. Cut a piece of thick paper or cardboard. Rip a rectangle from some brown wrapping paper and glue it in the middle.

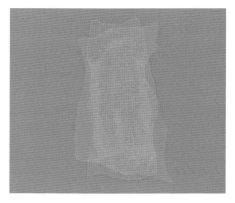

2. Rip a slightly wider rectangle from a bright piece of tissue paper and glue it over the brown wrapping paper.

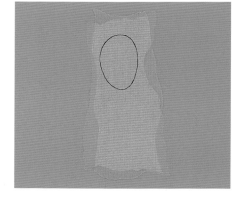

3. When the glue has dried, use a water-based felt-tip pen or a fountain pen to draw an oval for the face.

4. Draw two lines for the neck and a round-necked T-shirt. Add lines for the arms, but don't worry about drawing hands.

5. Draw a curved line for the eyebrow and nose, then add the other eyebrow and eyes. Draw the ears, hair and lips.

6. Then, dip a paintbrush into some clean water. Paint the water along some of the lines to make the ink run a little.

7. Rip a rough T-shirt shape from tissue paper and glue it over your drawing. Add a torn paper stripe, too.

8. Finally, when the glue has dried, paint thin stripes across the T-shirt using a bright shade of watery paint.

3-D bugs

Pinch the legs to
make them bend.

1. Cut out the middle and lower parts of a bug's body from textured paper. Glue the pieces onto some thick paper or cardboard.

2. Cut out a dome-shaped head and two eyes, and glue them on. Also cut out and glue on yellow shapes to fit on the body.

3. Cut out and glue on two lower wings. Cut four legs. Glue on the ends nearest the body. Pinch them in the middle.

The bug below is the one described in the steps.

Pull the folded ends out to make it stand up.

4. Cut out two more wings from tracing paper or tissue paper. Pinch each narrow end to make a fold. Glue on that end only.

5. For the ridges down the body, cut a strip of paper. Fold each end inward, then fold the ends back on themselves.

This orange bug has three sets of wings cut from textured paper.

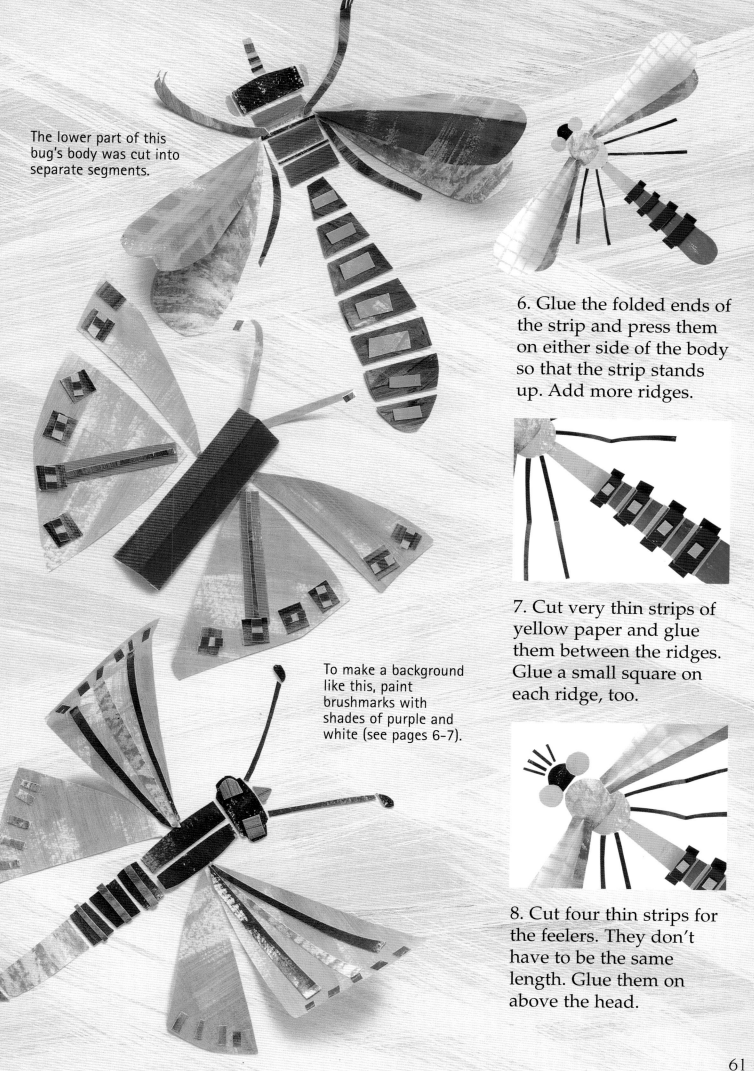

The lower part of this bug's body was cut into separate segments.

To make a background like this, paint brushmarks with shades of purple and white (see pages 6–7).

6. Glue the folded ends of the strip and press them on either side of the body so that the strip stands up. Add more ridges.

7. Cut very thin strips of yellow paper and glue them between the ridges. Glue a small square on each ridge, too.

8. Cut four thin strips for the feelers. They don't have to be the same length. Glue them on above the head.

Punched holes

BRIGHT PAPER OR TEXTURED PAPER (SEE PAGES 6-9)

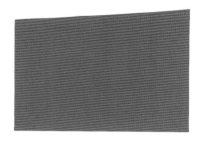

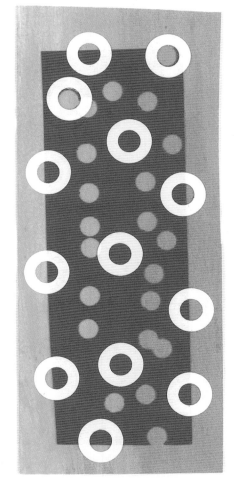

1. Cut a rectangle from bright or textured paper. The sides don't have to be exactly the same length.

2. Cut two strips from a contrasting shade of paper. Then, use a hole puncher to punch a row of holes along them.

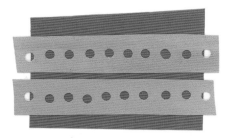

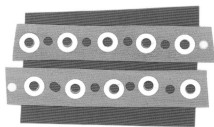

3. Lay the strips on some newspaper and spread glue on the back of each one. Then, press them onto the rectangle.

4. Press a reinforcing ring around alternate holes along the strips, to create a pattern of rings and punched holes.

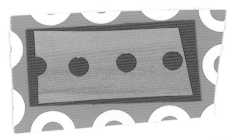

Experiment with different patterns of rings and where you punch holes in the paper.

The instructions below show you how to make this kind of pattern.

You can also add the punched-out circles from inside a hole puncher.

1. To make the example above, cut a rectangle of blue paper. Then, cut another, slightly smaller, purple rectangle.

Use a craft knife.

2. Press reinforcing rings onto the purple rectangle. Then, cut a small rectangle out of the middle of the paper, through the rings.

Glue the small rectangle in the middle.

3. Trim a little piece off each side of the small rectangle. Then, glue the pieces of purple paper onto the blue paper.

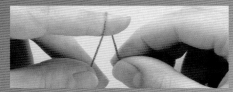  

Simple stitches

Stitches can be used to decorate not only material, but paper and cardboard too. These pages show you how to do some simple stitches and how to tie a knot to secure the thread before you start to stitch.

Tying a knot

Hold your nail tightly against your thumb as you pull.

1. Hold the end of a piece of thread between your thumb and first finger. Wrap the thread around your finger once.

2. Rub your finger hard along your thumb. You should feel the thread rolling and twisting between them.

3. Put your middle fingernail at the top of the rolled thread. Pull the long end of the thread hard and make a knot.

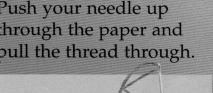

Running stitch

1. Thread a needle, then make a knot in one end. Push your needle up through the paper and pull the thread through.

2. Push the point of the needle down through the paper, a little way away. Then, pull the needle through from the back.

3. Push the needle up again a little way from your first stitch, then push it down again, pulling the thread tight.

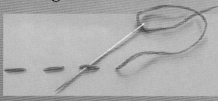 

4. Continue pushing the needle upwards and downwards in the same way, so that you make a line of stitches.

5. To finish off, stitch through the last stitch you made and pull the thread tight. Then, stitch through it again.

6. Push your needle through these stitches again, two more times. Then, cut the thread a little way away from the knot.

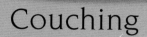

Wrapping

1. Cut a thin strip of cardboard or fabric. Thread a needle, then push it up through the strip, from the back.

2. Wrap the thread around and around the strip so that you cover a section of it. Pull the thread tight as you wrap.

3. When you have wrapped enough, stitch through the knot on the back two or three times to finish off.

Couching

1. Cut a piece of thick thread and lay it where you want to stitch it. Push your needle up from the back, next to the thread.

2. Push the needle down on the other side of the thread to make a small straight stitch. This will secure the thick thread.

This is the back.

3. Continue making small stitches over the thicker thread along its length. Finish off on the back with one or two stitches.

Sewing on a sequin and a bead

You will need to use a fine needle for this.

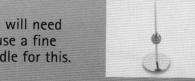

1. Push your needle up through the paper or fabric, but don't pull it all the way through. Slide a sequin onto the needle.

2. Slide a bead on top and pull the thread through both of them. Then, push the needle back through the hole in the sequin.

3. Pull the needle right through to the back of the paper or fabric. Then, tie a knot with the two ends of the thread.

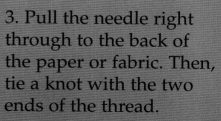

Stitched paper squares

CORRUGATED CARDBOARD AND TEXTURED PAPER (SEE PAGES 6-9)

Don't glue the small rectangles on.

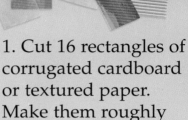

1. Cut 16 rectangles of corrugated cardboard or textured paper. Make them roughly the same size.

2. Rip a rectangle from tissue paper and glue it on one rectangle. Cut out two small squares from cardboard and paper.

3. Thread a needle and make a knot in the end. Holding all the pieces in place, stitch a bead in the middle of the squares.

Find how to finish off in steps 5 and 6 on page 64.

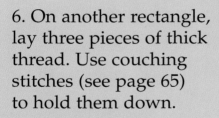

4. Then, stitch up through a rectangle of cardboard and one of textured paper. Wrap the thread around them several times.

5. As you are wrapping, push the needle through some beads and onto the thread. Wrap the thread again, then finish off.

6. On another rectangle, lay three pieces of thick thread. Use couching stitches (see page 65) to hold them down.

See page 64 for running stitches.

7. Lay a sequin on another rectangle, then put a piece of tissue paper on top. Use running stitches to stitch around the sequin.

8. Decorate the rest of the rectangles using the stitches on pages 64-65. The picture opposite shows lots of ideas.

9. When all the rectangles are decorated, use strong glue to stick them in rows on a large piece of thick paper.

Food collage

PIECES OF PAPER TEXTURED WITH PAINT (SEE PAGES 6-9)

1. Glue a piece of blue paper and a piece of textured paper across a large rectangle of purple paper, like this.

2. Cut two rectangles of checked paper from an old magazine, or draw some with felt-tip pens. Glue them at the top.

Add black marks on the bun.

3. For the burger bun, cut two orange shapes from textured paper. Cut an oval for the burger and two shapes for tomatoes.

4. Draw slices of onion with a blue pencil. Fill them in with blue paint. Draw some green lettuce, too. Cut out the shapes.

5. Glue the lettuce onto the bottom bun shape. Then, glue on the tomatoes, burger, onion, then the top bun shape.

Cut the straw in two and glue it on at an angle.

6. For the drink, cut out a beaker. Glue on a white oval and a smaller oval inside, for the drink. Paint a striped straw.

7. Cut a circle from green paper. Then, paint a lighter green circle in the middle. Glue on orangey-yellow strips for the french fries.

Cut out a foil lid for the carton.

8. Draw a plastic carton on a piece of white paper. Paint a red oval inside for the ketchup. Glue on a french fry.

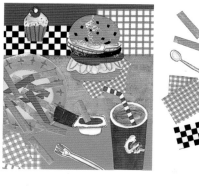

9. Glue all the things you have made onto the large piece of paper. Add other things, such as knives, forks, cakes and napkins.

Glittery branches

KITCHEN FOIL AND TRACING PAPER OR WHITE TISSUE PAPER

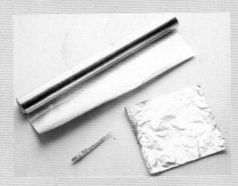

Bend and twist the branch, too.

1. Tear a wide strip of kitchen foil from a roll, then rip it in half. Scrunch one of the pieces of foil as tightly as you can.

2. Scrunch the other piece of foil tightly, too. Then, bend and twist both pieces to make wiggly twig shapes.

3. Tear another wider strip of foil and rip it in half. Scrunch it tightly around the ends of the two twigs to hold them together.

Make lots of branches and arrange them in a vase or lay them on a mantelpiece.

4. Repeat steps 1-3 to make another branch. Then, join the two branches together with another piece of foil.

You'll get two identical leaves.

5. Fold a piece of tracing paper or tissue paper in half. Draw a simple leaf shape. Then, cut it out, keeping the paper folded.

6. Spread glue on one leaf and press the end of a twig onto it. Lay the other leaf on top, sandwiching the twig between them.

7. Cut out more pairs of leaves and glue them around the ends of all the twigs in the same way. Then, let the glue dry.

8. Brush both sides of the leaves with white glue. Sprinkle the glue with glitter, then shake off any excess, when it is dry.

71

Cityscape

ANY TYPE OF PAPER OR CARDBOARD

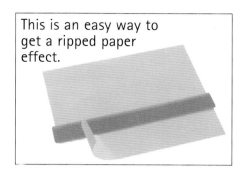

1. For the road, lay a ruler on a piece of paper. Press firmly on the ruler and rip the paper along its edge.

2. Glue the road along the bottom of a large piece of paper. Rip another piece, with an angle at one end, and glue it on.

3. For the buildings, rip rectangles from lots of different kinds of paper. Rip tower shapes on one end of some of them.

Use different types of paper, such as brown wrapping paper, or old envelopes.

4. Arrange the rectangles of paper along the road, then glue them on. Overlap some of them to get a 3-D effect.

5. Cut out and glue lots of windows on some of the buildings. Glue some strips of white tissue paper on some, too.

6. Draw an outline around a few of the buildings with a black felt-tip pen. Draw windows on some of them, too.

Draw some tiny cars. This helps to make the buildings look massive.

This tree was made
from two different
wrapping papers.

You could make
a tree from four
circles, like the
pink one above.

Dangling Christmas trees

WRAPPING PAPER

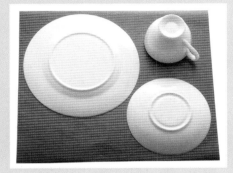

1. Draw around three circular objects of different sizes on a piece of wrapping paper. Then, cut out the circles.

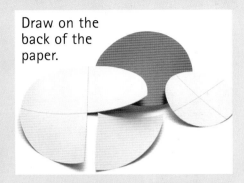

Draw on the back of the paper.

2. Roughly divide each circle into quarters, then cut a quarter from each one. You don't need the quarters you have cut out.

Cut about halfway up the cone.

3. Bend the largest circle around to make a cone and glue it together. Then, make lots of cuts around the bottom edge.

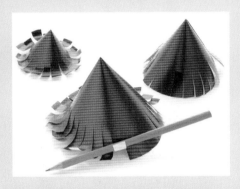

4. Roll each strip you have cut around a pencil, to make it curl. Make cones from the other two circles. Cut and curl them, too.

5. Thread a needle onto a long piece of thread. Make a big knot in one end. Push the needle up through the big cone.

6. Push the cone down as far as the knot. Make another knot a little further up the thread, then add the middle cone.

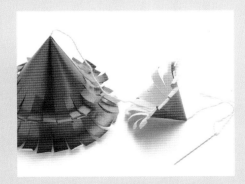

7. Push the middle cone down onto the second knot. Then, make a final knot and thread the smallest cone onto it.

8. Press a star sticker on either side of the thread at the top of the tree, or cut out and glue on stars or large flat sequins.

9. If you have used plain wrapping paper, you could decorate the trees with dots of glitter glue or tiny stickers.

Foil fish

THICK PAPER AND KITCHEN FOIL

The drops of water and the salt make the ink spread.

1. For the sea, mix turquoise ink with water, then use a thick brush to paint it all over a piece of thick paper.

2. Use the tip of the brush to dab on undiluted ink, then drop blobs of water onto it. Sprinkle salt all over, then let it dry.

3. For the sky, mix even more water with the turquoise ink and paint it all over another piece of thick paper.

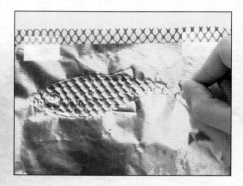

4. While the sky is still wet, dab on darker ink in a few places. Then, dab it with a tissue to lift off some of the ink.

5. While the backgrounds are drying, draw a simple fish shape on a piece of kitchen foil. Tape it to a net vegetable bag.

6. Use your thumbnail to rub the foil, inside the outline of the fish. The pattern of the net will show on the foil.

Leave the foil taped to the net.

7. Fill in a stripe of green felt-tip pen along the back of the fish. Add a light green stripe under it, then fill in below with yellow.

For the best effect, use felt-tip pens with permanent ink.

8. Draw purple and orange lines on the head. Add an eye with a black pen. Cut out the fish, then make several more.

9. Brush the salt off the sea, then cut a wavy line across it. Glue the sea onto the sky, then add the fish on top.

The salt reacts with the ink to leave these watery patterns.

Collage book covers

ANY TYPE OF PAPER

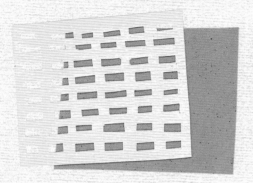

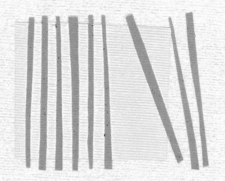

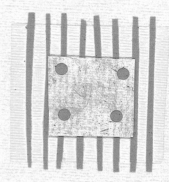

1. Use a craft knife to cut rows of little rectangles into a square of cream paper. Glue it onto a square of darker paper.

2. Then, use scissors to cut lots of thin strips of light brown paper and glue them onto a square of cream paper.

3. Use a hole puncher to punch holes into a paper square. Glue it onto brown paper, then glue them both on top of the strips.

The cream paper used in these squares is wallpaper.

Trim here. ———

4. Cut a 'spiral' in a paper square. Glue it at an angle onto some darker paper. Then, trim off any paper which overlaps the edge.

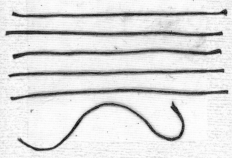

You could use these for the cover of a diary or photo album.

5. Cut several pieces of thick thread. Paint them with white glue, then press them in lines across a paper square.

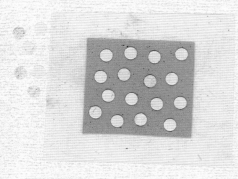

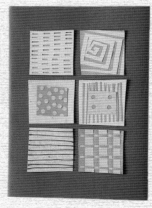

6. Decorate another square with circles from a hole puncher. Then, decorate one more using the ideas shown below.

7. Cut a piece of paper to the height of the book you want to cover. Make it long enough to fold inside the cover.

8. Lay the decorated squares in the middle of the book cover. Glue them on with strong glue, then leave it to dry.

More ideas

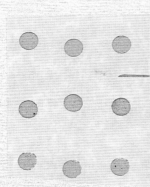

Include a square from a scrap of handmade paper, if you have any.

Fold some paper several times, then punch lines of holes in it.

Cut squares of different sizes and glue them on top of each other.

Add a small piece of paper weaving (see pages 26-27).

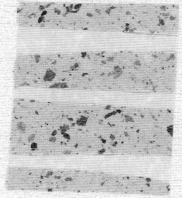

Cut strips of patterned paper and glue them on.

Rip strips of paper and glue them on top of each other.

Glue on lots of little paper squares at different angles.

Pierce lots of holes with an old ballpoint pen or a blunt needle.

3-D cityscape

THIN WHITE CARDBOARD

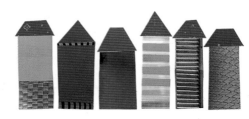

1. For the buildings, cut rectangles of patterned paper from magazines. Glue them onto a strip of thin white cardboard.

2. Cut out and glue on a roof for each building. Make some of them pointed and others flat on top.

3. Cut out windows, chimneys and doors, and glue them on. Try to find paper with squared or lined patterns on them.

4. For the road, cut strips of blue shades of paper. Glue them on in front of the buildings. Add white lines, too.

5. To protect your collage and make it stronger, you could cover it with clear book covering film, but you don't have to.

6. Use a craft knife to cut around the buildings and the road. Leave a border of white cardboard around them.

Bend it between your fingers and thumbs.

7. To curve the street so that it stands up, hold it in the middle. Move your hands outwards, bending it slightly as you go.

8. Make more streets in the same way. Make one without a road in front, then others which are taller than the first street.

9. Cut out metallic-looking papers for skyscrapers. Make them from several pieces of paper glued on top of each other.

Finish the cityscape with a road and hedges.

Assemble the streets one behind the other. You could press a small piece of poster tack on the back to secure them.

81

Shiny paper garland

SCRAPS OF WRAPPING PAPER

1. Cut a very long piece of ribbon. Then, fold a piece of wrapping paper in half and cut out a circle, through both layers.

2. Spread glue on one of the circles and lay the ribbon on top. Then, press on the other circle, matching the edges.

3. Cut lots of circles from different wrapping papers and glue them along the ribbon. Leave small spaces in between them.

Some of these garlands had triangles glued onto them, as well as circles and stars.

4. In some places, press the ribbon onto a star sticker, then add another sticker on top, matching the edges.

5. When you have filled the ribbon with shapes, decorate some of the plain circles by gluing on little sequins.

These garlands look effective hanging vertically, with pieces of ribbon hanging between them.

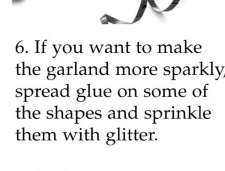

6. If you want to make the garland more sparkly, spread glue on some of the shapes and sprinkle them with glitter.

Tissue paper windows

TISSUE PAPER

1. Rip about fifteen strips of bright tissue paper. Make some of them the same length and width.

2. Using a glue stick, glue the edge of one of the strips. Then, press another strip onto the glue.

3. Continue gluing and overlapping different strips until you've made a rectangle.

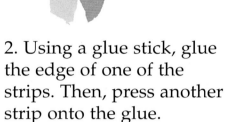

Tape the tissue paper to a window to get the full effect.

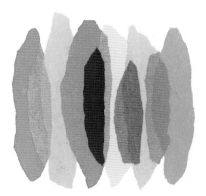

4. Glue some smaller contrasting strips on top. Make them overlap the edges of the long strips.

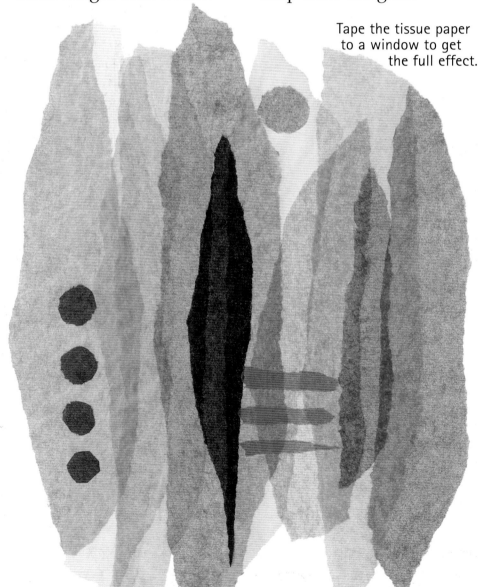

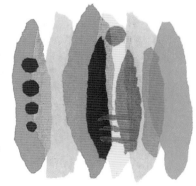

5. Rip different sizes of spots and glue them on. Glue on some little horizontal strips, too.

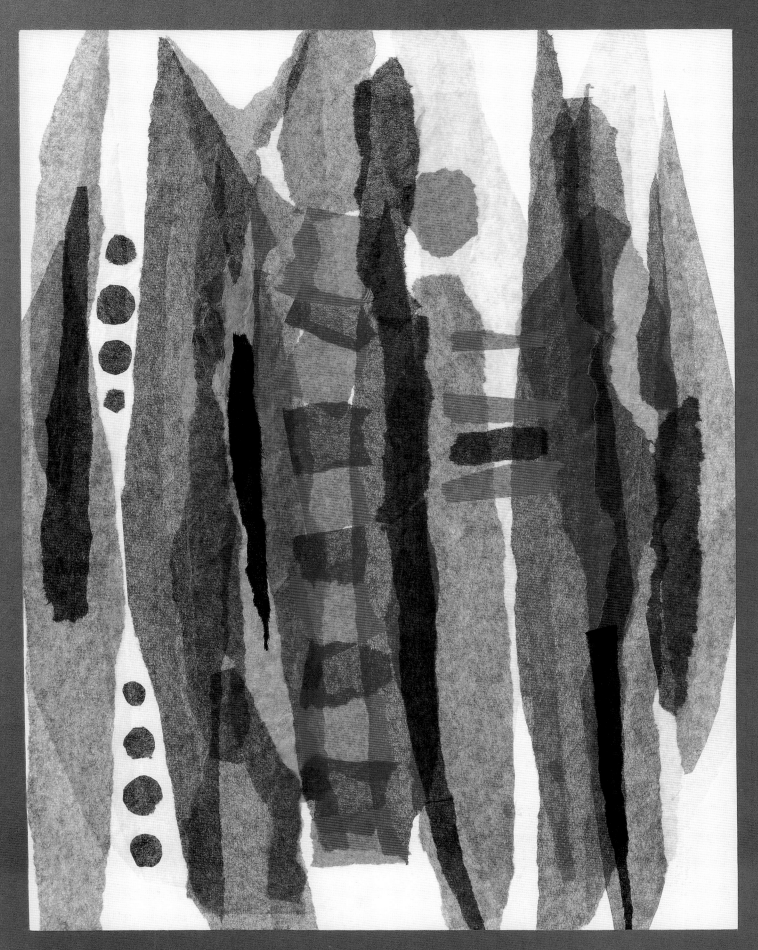

Glue the ends of the strips to the back of a simple frame (see pages 54–57) and lean it against a window.

Collage cards
WRAPPING PAPER, CARDBOARD AND BRIGHT PAPER

All these cards were made using the same technique. Some of them had extra shapes glued on top.

To make a row of triangles like this, cut 'v' shapes and fold them back.

1. Cut a rectangle of paper for the front of the card. Then, cut two smaller rectangles from paper or thin cardboard.

This makes the inside a different shade to the front.

2. For the card itself, cut a rectangle of blue paper and fold it in half. Glue the largest rectangle on top and trim the edges.

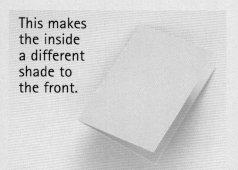

3. Glue the smallest paper rectangle onto the back of a piece of shiny paper or wrapping paper, then trim around it.

4. Then, use a craft knife to cut five lines which cross each other near the top of the paper. Push a pencil through the cuts.

5. Gently fold each part back and crease them, so that the shiny paper makes a shape on the front of the paper.

6. Glue the pieces of paper onto the card. Then, use a gold pen to draw a pattern in the folded-back shape.

Bright paper windows

CREAM OR ANOTHER PALE SHADE OF PAPER

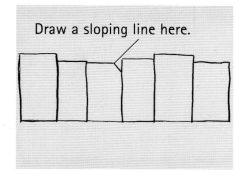

Draw a sloping line here.

1. Draw several rectangles across the middle of the paper with a dip pen and black ink, or a felt-tip pen.

2. Draw simple patterns for roof tiles on some of the buildings. Add more details such as chimneys.

3. Draw windows and doors. Copy some of the styles of windows from the big picture below.

Place your picture against a window. The light will glow through the tissue paper.

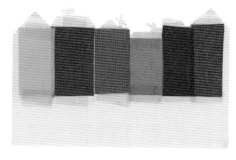

4. Use a craft knife to cut roughly around the top of the buildings. Cut out the windows, too.

5. Cut strips of tissue paper the width of each building and tape them to the back of the picture.

6. Turn the picture over and glue a piece of light blue tissue paper along the bottom for a canal.

You could draw some striped posts on the canal.

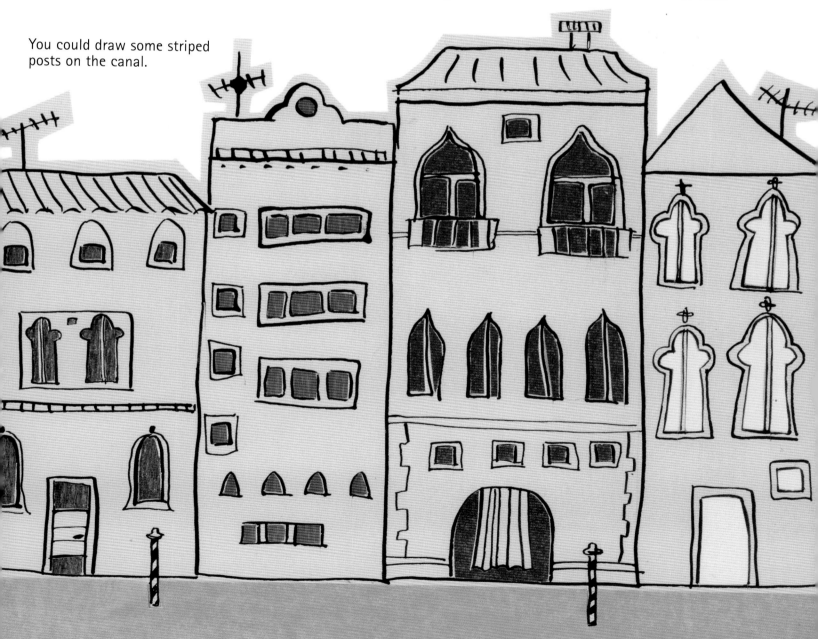

Paper crocodile

BRIGHT ART PAPER

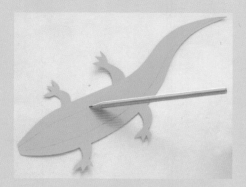

1. Draw a simple outline of a crocodile on thick paper and cut it out. Then, draw two wavy lines along its back.

2. Score along the lines by running a craft knife gently over the paper, without cutting all the way through.

3. Erase the pencil lines. Then, cut some teeth on either side of the wavy lines. Cut two large crosses for eyes.

4. Turn it over and cut small crosses along the back, between the wavy lines. Score a curve where each leg meets the body.

5. Push a pencil gently into each cross. Use the pencil to push up the eyes and the teeth, too. Turn the crocodile over.

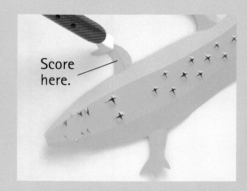

Score here.

6. To shape the body, pinch along the wavy lines to crease them. Score along the legs and feet then crease them, too.

7. To make the water for the picture, score a wavy line along a piece of blue paper. Carefully crease along the scored line.

8. Turn the paper over and score another wavy line, following the shape of the first one. Then, crease this line.

9. Continue to score and fold lines on alternate sides of the paper. Then, cut a wavy line along the top of the paper.

Score the green paper on alternate sides.

10. For the background, score wavy lines on green paper. Then, cut a curve in some yellow paper and score a wavy line along it.

11. Cut long shapes for the grass at the bottom. Score and crease a curving line down the middle of each shape.

12. Arrange all the pieces. Then, put tiny dots of glue on the back of each piece and glue them gently together.

Town collage

THICK PAPER OR CARDBOARD

1. Make a rough plan for your collage on a piece of scrap paper. Mark on the position of roads, a park, buildings, cars, and so on.

2. On a large piece of paper or cardboard, paint the shapes which are the roads on your plan, with acrylic or poster paint.

3. For the park, rip pieces from light shades of paper in old magazines and glue them on. Add green paper for grass.

4. Fill in the areas for the buildings with dark pieces of paper. Rip shapes for the buildings and add some windows.

5. For the cars, rip a shape for the body, with wheel arches ripped out. Glue two wheels behind and windows on top.

6. For a cat, rip the body from magazine paper which has a texture on it. Glue on paws. Cut out an eye and glue it on, too.

The shapes in this collage were glued on at different angles to give it a topsy-turvy effect.

7. For the people, rip all the parts of the body and the clothes. Glue the pieces together, then glue them onto the collage.

Decorated gift boxes

PICTURES FROM MAGAZINES AND WRAPPING PAPERS

The glue goes transparent when it dries.

1. Rip or cut out pictures from old magazines. Rip pieces from wrapping paper too, or decorate your own (see below).

2. Glue the pieces of paper all over a cardboard box, such as an old chocolate box. Glue them so that they overlap.

3. When the box is covered, brush white glue all over. This helps to protect the box and makes it stronger.

Ideas for pieces to glue on

Use a brown felt-tip, or ink and a dip pen, to write long lines of joined-up writing on cream paper.

Rip old-fashioned black and white or sepia photographs of people from old magazines.

Cut or rip stamps and printed postmarks from envelopes and packages and glue them on.

To make paper look old, leave a teabag in water for a few minutes, then wipe it across the paper.

Cut small stars from bright paper and glue them on, or stick on gummed paper stars.

Paint watery ink across pieces of newspaper or use a teabag to stain it (see far left).

Index